D1275826

Copyright © 2000 by Nord-Süd Verlag AG, Gossau Zürich, Switzerland
First published in Switzerland under the title *Das Geheimnis der Bären*
English translation copyright © 2000 by North-South Books Inc.

All rights reserved. No part of this book may be reproduced or utilized in any form or by any means, electronic or mechanical, including photocopying, recording, or any information storage and retrieval system, without permission in writing from the publisher.

First published in the United States, Great Britain, Canada, Australia, and New Zealand in 2000 by North-South Books, an imprint of Nord-Süd Verlag AG, Gossau Zürich, Switzerland. Distributed in the United States by North-South Books Inc., New York.

Library of Congress Cataloging-in-Publication Data is available.
A CIP catalogue record for this book is available from The British Library.
ISBN 0-7358-1363-9 (trade binding) 10 9 8 7 6 5 4 3 2 1
ISBN 0-7358-1364-7 (library binding) 10 9 8 7 6 5 4 3 2 1
Printed in Italy

For more information about our books, and the authors and artists who create them, visit our web site: www.northsouth.com

E c. 1

The Bears' Christmas Surprise

From a story by Bruno Hächler
Adapted and translated by J. Alison James
Illustrated by Angela Kehlenbeck

A Michael Neugebauer Book
NORTH-SOUTH BOOKS / NEW YORK / LONDON

DISCARD
STAUNTON PUBLIC LIBRARY

It was Christmas Eve. A bear with a red bow tie sat forgotten on the bookshelf. He had been there for years. Hours of play and then neglect had made his fur dull and shaggy. But the corner of his eyes still held the glow from the time when he first was clasped in a child's arms. He had been a Christmas present that day. He was the first bear to disappear.

Quietly he made his way outside. He shivered in the cold winter wind. But he just hunched up his shoulders and set off, determined. When he reached the abandoned shed, he waited.

From everywhere around the town the other bears slipped away. They tiptoed out of children's rooms, squeezed out of toy chests, and climbed down from shop window displays.

One after another they came—fleecy bears with friendly faces, elegant bears, and delicate bears, bears with frizzy fur and velvet fur, and an odd-looking tiny one in an angel costume—an endless stream.
Just as they were all assembled, the bells in the church tower struck midnight.

Satisfied, the first bear looked around.
Not a single bear was missing. He nodded silently.
That was the sign.
The bears burst outside and spread throughout the town,
eager to begin their work.

Silently they climbed
over fences and balconies,
slid down chimneys and
crawled through cat
flaps. They headed
straight for the
presents that were
wrapped and ready
for Christmas morning.

Swiftly the bears untied every bow. They slipped off the wrapping paper and removed each gift. Then they wrote little notes in their squiggly bear writing, put them into the boxes, and wrapped them up again.
They found lovely things: bottles of perfume, building blocks, ice skates, model tractors, and drawing pencils. They put these things into their backpacks and bags and took them to other houses. It was the bears' surprise.

Just before dawn, when the bears had finished, they returned to their places in children's rooms, toy chests, and shop windows.

The glad cries of Christmas were mute that morning. When children opened their empty boxes, they wept with disappointment. Their parents saw the little notes and ran next door for help, but in each house it was the same story. The presents were all gone, and no one knew where.

The people sat for a long time, doing nothing, for what was Christmas without presents? Then it occurred to them to see what was written on the mysterious notes.

At first they didn't understand. But they read the messages once more, and then again. And each time, their hearts pounded more swiftly and their disappointment melted away.

"This package is as empty as my arms."

"My heart remembers when you ran to me with joy."

"I am longing for a cheerful visit."

"Do you remember me? I often think of you."

And suddenly they thought of the many lonely people in the city. In the notes, they heard the voices of people they knew, but had forgotten. How awful to be forgotten and alone on Christmas Day.

Swiftly they pulled
on their warmest
clothes and set out.

They visited the grandmother in the nursing home, the aunt who sat alone by the window, the man who missed his own family terribly. Not a single person in the city was overlooked.

And in each home they visited, they found mysterious packages: games and toys and warm mittens and perfume. The lonely people of the town celebrated a Christmas with gifts and company and holiday cheer.

Soon laughter and music rang from brightly lit windows.
Over and over the same phrase was heard,
"Merry Christmas!"

The next night, the bears who slept alone—those that were left behind on shelves, in toy boxes, or in the shops—these bears were called back to the abandoned shed. To their surprise, they found a great tree, hung with glowing candles. Under its arching branches lay a pile of presents, one for each bear. And for that long night, the bears forgot their loneliness and played until morning.

When the bear with the red bow tie climbed back to his place on the shelf, he looked a little more tattered than before. But his eyes gleamed more than ever, because of the bears' Christmas surprise.